THE Boy Who Would Be King

First published in the United Kingdom
by HarperCollins *Children's Books* in 2023
HarperCollins *Children's Books* is a division of
HarperCollins *Publishers* Ltd
1 London Bridge Street, London SE1 9GF

www.harpercollins.co.uk

HarperCollins *Publishers*
Macken House, 39/40 Mayor Street Upper
Dublin 1, D01 C9W8, Ireland

1 3 5 7 9 10 8 6 4 2

ISBN 978-0-00-861540-6

MIX
Paper from
responsible sources
FSC™ C007454

FSC
www.fsc.org

michael morpurgo

THE Boy Who Would Be King

illustrated by

Michael Foreman

HarperCollins *Children's Books*

Foreword

Just a short time ago I wrote a fairy tale inspired by the life of our late Queen Elizabeth the Second. I called it *There Once Is a Queen*. She had been queen almost all my life. As a young boy, I saw her coronation live on a small black-and-white television in my village hall, the whole village gathered round. I grew up knowing her as queen, all through my childhood, my teenage years, grown-up years, years as a family man, husband, father, grandfather, great-grandfather. And all my life she was there. Sadly, sadly, she died shortly after I wrote my fairy story.

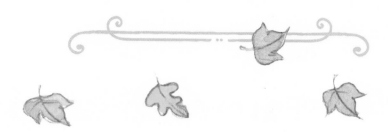

And now we have a new king, shortly to be crowned, her son, King Charles the Third. He is just a little younger than me, but he was a boy when I was a boy. We grew up part of the same generation. I always felt a kinship. He, like me, went away to boarding school, and he, like me, developed an abiding love of nature and the countryside.

I thought I might write another fairy story, very much inspired by King Charles, and by his childhood in particular.

Michael Foreman — who is the wonderful illustrator of both these books — and I, should like to dedicate this book to His Majesty the King, and Her Majesty the Queen Consort, wishing them well and happy in the years ahead.

There once was a boy

who was different,

not like other children.

He knew it and other children knew it.

Everyone knew it,

that he was going to be king one day,

when he was older.

He lived with his family in a great palace, with high walls and fences all around. He was never allowed out, not on his own. Sometimes, looking out of his window, it felt to him like a prison.

His mummy and daddy were forever busy doing what queens and kings do, meeting the people, shaking hands, opening this school and that hospital, even launching ships. He didn't really know much about what they did. He just knew it kept them away from him, and he didn't like that. They always seemed to be going off somewhere, or coming back, but not staying.

There were always people in the palace to look after him. His nanny looked after him, and she was always kind to him, as kind as anyone could be, but, even so, he often felt very alone in the world, and sad.

But when they came home, when they stopped being
King and Queen and became Mummy and Daddy again, they
would sometimes take him for long walks in the countryside,
with the dogs or the horses,
and he loved that.

They loved what he loved, the wind in the trees, the glimpse of a deer or a fox, the river rushing by, a fish rising, the heron in the shallows, the darting kingfisher, the ducks taking off noisily, watching the sun setting over the hills, then a pale moon rising, stomping home in the evening through muddy fields in wellies,

his pockets full of shining acorns and conkers.

All these they loved together.

Soon he had a new sister, and at last someone to play with at home, someone he could explore with, play hide-and-seek with. So he wasn't lonely any more. Once he ran off down the corridor into the Throne Room and hid under one of the thrones. His sister soon gave up looking for him, but no one told him. The dogs found him in the end, hours later, curled up fast asleep under the throne. His daddy said afterwards it was the best thing

you could do with a throne:

go to sleep under it.

These were the happiest times,

when the boy and his sister were together,

playing games, running wild outside, picking blackberries,

cleaning out the stables, looking after the horses,

just having fun. Happiest times,

best times.

But then came the worst times. He was on a walk with his daddy in the countryside. But he could see his daddy wasn't happy, wasn't telling him as usual about the trees or the badger setts, wasn't listening out for the cuckoo or the blackbird. He wasn't talking at all, and that was unusual, strange.

After a while, his daddy sat him down in their favourite place, on the trunk of an old oak tree.

He still said nothing for a while.

And then he told him.

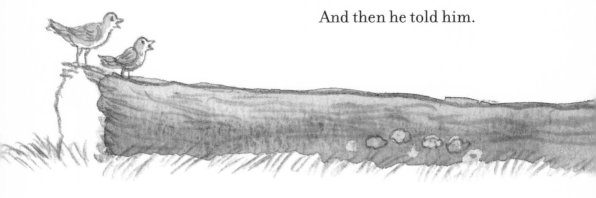

"You won't like what I have to tell you," he said, "but
Mummy and I, we think the time has come for you to leave
home, and go away to boarding school, like most boys do, like
I did. You're old enough now. You're a prince. You're going to
be a king. There's a lot you're going to have to do that you may
not like. Time to grow up. Don't worry. You'll love it there.
You'll make lots of new friends, have lots of fun. There's a
park to play in, trees to climb. You'll play sports."

As he told him, his daddy looked as sad
as the boy felt inside.

His mummy looked just as sad when they got back
to the palace, his sister too. It felt to the boy like
the end of the world.

The day the boy dreaded came all too soon.
They dressed him up in a grey uniform, took him off to
the school, which was in a big house in the countryside,
where all the boys were dressed in grey and wore grey
caps and the teachers had grey unsmiling faces —

"masters", they were called.

They wore black gowns and seemed to smoke pipes, most
of them. His bed in the dormitory sagged in the middle, the
food was horrible — especially the stew and the lumpy rice
pudding — but they always had to eat all of it. They made you
sit there until you did. And you had to have a cold bath after
sports. The matron who looked after them was as strict as
the masters, and had thin lips
that never smiled.

The boy was homesick and often cried himself to sleep at night, but he cried quietly to himself so the other boys would not hear him, because he knew that if they did they'd call him names and laugh at him.

He didn't make friends easily because he was new to school ways, and shy, and because of who he was. Some of the other boys teased him because everyone knew he was the boy who would be king one day. All he could think of was how much he hated this place and how much he wanted

to go home.

There were lessons — endless, dreary lessons — and tests, and cross-country runs, which he hated. It was on one of these runs that the boy made up his mind he would do it.

He would run away.

He would go home — how, he didn't know — and tell them he was never going back.

It was easy. On the next cross-country run, he ran even slower than usual till he was sure there was no one else behind him. Then he stopped and crouched down, pretending his shoelace had come undone and needed tying, just in case a master came looking for him.

He watched the others all disappear into the distance.

Then he took off into the woods and ran.

He had no idea where he was going.

He didn't mind as long as it was away from school.

The woods became deeper, but on he ran.

The woods became darker, but on he ran. He felt cold now, cold right through. He couldn't feel his feet. Then through the trees he could see a light ahead, a flickering light. He could smell smoke.

He came out of the woods and into a clearing
where there was a wooden shack, with one window
and a chimney. There were lots of hens clucking about
outside, and a pond with ducks upended in the water.
There was a goat too, with a long beard,
that looked up, eyed him
and then went back to eating a carrot.

The old woman who came out to feed the
chickens didn't seem in the least surprised to see him.

"Lost, are you?" she said. "You're shivering yourself
to death. Come in by the stove. Come along in, boy.
I'm not a witch, won't eat you. Come along." She
looked a bit like the boy's granny, a bit strict to look at,
but with a gentle voice.
And he was cold,
as cold as he'd ever been.

She hung up his clothes to dry, wrapped him in a blanket and sat him in front of the stove where he shivered the cold out of himself, his hands tight round a mug of hot soup. She was talking to him all the while about the dog that lay like a great shaggy carpet at the boy's feet, looking up at him.

"Prince, I call him," she said, "because he's brave and kind and true and, best of all, he never lets me down — he's just as a prince should be."

"You'll be hungry," she went on. "Lucky for you,
I was making some cakes." And she busied herself for a
while with her cakes before putting them in the oven.

"I've got to go out and shut the hens up, in case the fox comes," she told him. "I may be a while. So you watch the cakes for me. Just have a look in the oven every once in a while and when they're nice and brown take them out. Can you do that?

Won't be long. Prince will look after you."

And out she went.

The boy tried to stay awake, but he couldn't. His eyes closed, and before he knew it he was away in his dreams. He was dreaming he was on a cross-country run, that he was running away from school. He dreamed of meeting a strange old woman, of sitting by the stove in her shack in the woods, of a dog called Prince, who was licking his face, trying to wake him up. He dreamed of smoke coming out of the oven, of the old woman trying to wake him. He opened his eyes and the cakes were there in front of him on the table, all out of the stove,

all of them black,

and the room full of smoke.

He knew his dream had come true. He'd burned the cakes. And the old woman was not pleased.

"You fell asleep," she said. "And that's a pity. A waste of good food. I don't like waste."

"I'm sorry," said the boy.

"Never mind," she said. "I've got eggs. I'll make you an omelette and while I do you can tell me all about yourself." She laughed. "There was a king once a long time ago, called Alfred, a good king too. Not a king by any chance, are you?"

"Sort of," said the boy, and then he told her his whole story, how unhappy he was, how he didn't ever want to

go back to that school,

or be a prince

or a king.

By the time he'd finished, they had eaten the omelette and become the best of friends. The old woman leaned forward and took his hands in hers. "I want to tell you something. That King Alfred I was telling you about, he was running away, just like you are, because just like you he had lost his courage. Hundreds of years ago it was. The Vikings had invaded and had beaten him in battle and were hunting him down.

He was hiding away in some old woman's cottage.
She'd left him there to watch the cakes she was baking
and he fell asleep. When he woke up,

the cakes were burnt.

"Well, the old woman was not at all happy, and told him just what she thought of him: that he was feeling sorry for himself, that he should wake his ideas up, stop burning people's cakes, get on with being king and drive those Vikings out of England. And do you know what he did? He went off and he gathered his army again and defeated those Vikings and drove them out of England.

"Then when he'd done that he set about trying to be the best king England had ever had. He wanted to change the lives of the people for the better. And do you know what he did? He made sure that as many of his people could read and write as possible, that as many children could go to school as possible, and learn.

He loved words, ideas, knowledge,
and wanted everyone to be able to
learn all they could.
What do you love?"

"Home," said the boy.

"I love to be home with my family.

And I love the birds, the wind, the sky, trees,

herons, kingfishers, otters,

mud, cows.

I love being in the countryside.

It's like my family. It's where I belong.

When I grow up, I want to help look after it, all of it."

"Maybe you'll be the new King Alfred, then," she told him. "He had a dream like you. Alfred ran away like you, once. But he went back, faced the world, faced the Vikings, beat them, drove them out of England. And then he set about making his dream come true. He loved reading, just as much as you love the countryside. Very few people could read in those days and he thought that was wrong, and he was going to put that right. There wouldn't be schools without King Alfred."

"You think I should go back
to school, don't you?"

"Yes," she said. "I do." They talked together for a long while, the two of them. The boy didn't want to leave at all. But he knew he had to, that she was right, that running away was not the answer. As he was leaving, she said, "Before you go, I've got a present for you." She reached into her pocket and gave him an acorn. "Plant it. Plant many trees.

Be a good king, like Alfred.

I know you will be."

It was strange. When the boy got back to school a while later, it was as if time had stood still. No one seemed to realise he'd been missing. They just thought that he'd come back last from the run, a long way behind, as usual. Yet he knew he'd been gone for hours.

Stranger still was that, time and again, over the years he tried to go to see the old woman again, to find the shack in the woods, with the one window and the chimney, with the duck pond and the hens. He never found it.

It was as if she'd never been there.

But she had been there.

He had the acorn to prove it.

He planted the acorn at home in the palace
gardens, watered it, protected it, tended it, loved it.
He watched it grow year after year.

     The acorn became a sapling,

          the sapling became a young tree.

The boy grew up too and became a
prince and in time the prince became
a king. He never forgot the old woman
in the woods, and burning her cakes.
He never forgot her wisdom and
kindness towards him.

Years and years later when the time came for the boy to be crowned king, there was a great coronation in the cathedral, and the trumpets sounded and the choir sang.

They put a crown on his head,

which was heavy.

As he rode in the coronation coach back to the palace afterwards, his beautiful wife beside him, the crowds cheering them all the way back to the palace, he wondered if it had all been a dream, his childhood, his schooldays, that day he'd run away, the old woman whose cakes he had burned.

She had shared with him her love of the world, had
given him courage, and helped to show him the
way, how he might become a king like Alfred, a king
who could help change the world for the better,
for the trees, the birds,
for all creatures great and small,
for everyone.

All through the coronation he had kept in his pocket an acorn from the tree that he had planted. He took it out now and showed it to his wife sitting beside him, who knew of course all about the oak tree and the old woman in the woods whose cakes her husband had burned, just like Alfred. He knew she loved that story.

"I'll do my best," he said to her.
"Like Alfred. Promise, promise."

"I know you will," she said.

$\mathcal{A}$nd both of them knew
the old lady in the woods
was there with them,
and listening.